The view f
A mystery
By Eric Thornton

Only if you have nothing else to do!

© Eric Thornton

This book is dedicated to Fallyn. You know what you did.

1

I don't want to think of the garbage that could come out of this town.

The only reason I'm here is that my parents are dead and they only wished for me to leave my hometown.

It is a sad shame to lose one's parents but it is what it is.

I get into the house with my one bag of shit.

That's all I have.

I didn't think to start grabbing other things but it is fine.

This town is something and a half.

Why I went from one small town to another is something I regret in retrospect.

These are the things I have problems with nosey ass people.

I walk through the house and once I get to the backyard, I see it: a corpse sitting fresh on my lawn.

Wonderful.

Guess I better call law enforcement.

After using my phone data to find out the number, I call it in and wait for them to show.

It is a small town. It shouldn't take long. I end up waiting 20 minutes. By this point, if someone would ask me what the very detail of the flesh would be, I would be able to give an excruciating reply.

I'm not a master of detail but damn if I wouldn't be able to share what I could find.

The poor woman. She looks like she has suffered a great deal of brutality.

Sores that look fresh to the point. Blood that has likely clotted by this point.

But strangely, none is pouring from her fresh flesh. Why would that be a thing?

Maybe I've read my fair share of novels but wouldn't that be truth and existence if one were fresh to be killed?

"Are you the one that called it in?" a raw in the throat kind of voice asks.

I jump at the sudden sound of it, relieved of the gravity for a moment or two as I place a hand on my somewhat round chest.

I'm not exactly rotund but at the same time, I'm also not that person that belongs on a billboard. I will say that much.

"I am," I remark and point to the body.

He nods and a crew walks through the house as if they own it when I am, in fact, a fresh owner of this residence. But given the misfortune of this house now becoming a crime scene, I guess I'm about to be stripped of my keys.

"What are you doing here?" he says in that rough voice once more.

And here I thought nosiness applied to everyone, not just special cases of people wanting to have gossip to share.

The keys, still fresh yet somehow bulky in my hand, are quickly snatched.

"Excuse you, would work," I remark at the wall of muscle that is the officer with the voice in need of a lozenge.

"So would manners on you. It seems they truly are a waste on the youth."

"The youth? Bitch, you have to be something of 23," I remark.

"I'm 39 but I do appreciate the compliment."

"What's with the snatching of my stuff?" I ask.

"You never did tell me what you are doing here," he replies.

As if I have no room or right to talk.

Clearly, someone needs to be knocked back a peg or two.

"I just bought this house. I'm moving in."

"Rather unfortunate," he mutters.

"Why? Because of the corpse? Or is there something more afoot here?"

"You are a curious one, aren't you?" He looks at me while stroking his ever so sharp chin. The man is a weapon in all forms.

"What makes you expect that?" I remark.

"I know nothing about you. How do I know you didn't just break into this place and claim it for your own?"

I whip out a set of pages folded like that of a paper fan. I hand them over with a slight smack and he glances over them. His eyes dart from left to right, over and over, reading it with such speed and urgency.

Almost like he is being timed.

"Seems like that is in order. Sadly the previous person that sold you the house is unable to be talked to."

"Why? Did they disconnect their phone or something?" I ask.

"Because you found her in the yard," he replies as he guides me out the front door with my singular bag.

2

"How are you so quick to identify a body without fingerprint analysis, blood match, or anything?"

"You read a lot of mysteries, don't you?"

"Actually no. I'm far too aware of common sense."

"What do you know of analysis then?"

"I know enough to know that you don't have the sense to know someone that quick."

He crosses his arms at me. How someone can have arms as stacked as his and not have tumors or large masses in them is beyond me.

But I refuse to be close to someone. I refuse to consider any prospect of affection. My sexuality--not a choice--has nothing to do with my view on him.

I see him as a brute and nothing more. Not that it would matter.

He is a coarse being of a rough personality. He is very abrasive and makes no attempt to hide it.

"This is a small town. And as someone that has been here most of my life, I know people. Did you research anything about our town before you moved in?"

"I didn't get that luxury," I clip at him.

"What do you mean?"

I question whether or not I should provide him any details about me or if that should be another mystery of its own.

"It doesn't matter."

"You do realize that makes you ever so suspicious to the sheriff of this town, right?"

Him? Sheriff?

He with the ego from hell and the button-down shirt with the sleeves rolled up with faded dark jeans. He with the ego from hell and the attitude to match.

I have never been harshly treated in my life.

Not that it would matter. People are corrosive and coarse as can be until they get the dirt they wish to uncover and discover from you or about you.

Then they tend to decide if you are worth their time or not.

People are very intriguing beings. Most are rough and borderline abusive with their looks, judgment, and the wagging of their tongues.

And it seems this is yet another town that does the same.

The petty suspicions. The various accusations. It is petty.

Cheap.

"Fine. I'll cast my mourning to you. I've lost my only family, my parents to the stages of their advanced lives. Their hearts stopped and I was given 2 weeks to get my shit and get out. I found a house--this one--in a week's time and made a move to it. The rest is history it seems." The deep, grave history that might or might not haunt me for the remainder of my days.

Whether or not it will be like this the rest of my life, I am unsure.

He looks at me with a sadness I've seen far too much in a short time. "My condolences."

"Take your condolences and do what you must. I only wish to have this house and make it my own."

"How about we reach a bargain?" he asks.

"Like what?"

"You avoid your backyard until I give the all-clear and you can take the time to move in. That work for you?"

"Don't you need fingerprints? Some time to test the house?"

"Nope."

Curious.

"Why not?"

"Because there was evidence that showed she was cast into the backyard over the fence."

Well played, sheriff. Make me the fool if you must.

3

I accept the terms and conditions that he has set up. I didn't plan on going into the backyard anyway. I would've kept it trimmed but nothing more.

"And what do I do about furniture?"

"I'll call some people to help get you some furniture. Are you the picky kind?" he asks.

It almost sounds like he is hitting on me, which I'm far from interested in. I don't care about having a romantic life.

I don't plan on worrying or wondering about that.

I'm more the person that would rather stick to hanging out on his own.

That's just me.

"Don't do me any favors. I'll figure something out," I remark.

"You have never been to a caring small town, have you?"

"This is the second small town I've been in my whole life. I grew up in one that I was born in and let's just say, they were more for the drama and the talk than anything. Any dirt was good dirt," I return.

"I'm sorry you faced that for so long in your life," he says.

"I'm not. It's turned me into the hardened person I've become."

"Maybe that is a problem that could be remedied."

"What are you getting at? I'm not exactly one for hovering and dancing to a tune that doesn't match a beat I care for."

He looks at me with a hint of a smile. "Let me put it this way. Welcome to the good part of society. Welcome to a town that cares about people more than it cares about materialism. We might be small but we do help each other out. We don't go seeking out gossip. We don't look for something to hang over someone's head. Anyone that does that here is clearly not from here and hasn't been raised with manners and kindness."

And yet he started off being abrasive as ever. Where is the truth in this town after that?

"So what makes you think it was okay to snatch keys from me and treat me so coldly?"

"We've had a few issues with people lately. Some people are coming in and trying to take over this town. Trying to knock people down. Use them. Scam them. Kidnap. We've dealt with some abrasive people lately and we don't take kindly to it."

"So you look at a man in his late twenties that has been loved and living with his

13

parents forever and assume he is out to start shit?"

"To be honest, most of the people that have started shit are around your age."

Wow.

Talk about being placed in a category.

"Well I'm sorry I fit into a box of bad people but role placing someone right off the bat doesn't exactly make for a warm welcome."

He scrubs his face with his hand for a moment.

I am someone that doesn't appreciate the way people subscribe to placing others inboxes. I'm not someone that ever wants to be put in a box of roles. I don't ever want to be labeled. To me, labels are cheap and petty.

There is no way for me to not feel that way. No one has ever proven me wrong.

It is hard to not be upset by that. It is not just on older generations, it is a mind-frame that people subscribe to. They see it, hear it, and instantly go to, "yes, this is acceptable" then carry it the rest of their days.

But when someone doesn't choose to be a sheep but rather a shepherd to a different flock and a future, it is frowned upon. It is seen as the black sheep situation all over again.

I, for one, will never be that person. I know that at my age, most suspect that I am going to change. That they can break me of having the free spirit mentality.

Good luck. I was raised by parents--universe rests their souls--that believed everyone could be good. Two people that continued to encourage the idea for their son to be different.

To be his own person rather than just another sheep in the flock.

And I'll be damned if I spit on their memory by becoming a sheep.

4
Next thing I know, less than an hour give or take, a group of people is heading for the house. Ones that are not part of the police squad as far as I know.

And honestly, I'm not sure how to feel about it.

Just how small is this town?

I grab my phone and glance at it.

I look up the town I'm in and look at the population. 80 people. This is something new.

The town I grew up in had a decent hundred to hundred and fifty people.

So this town is a little smaller. But I am curious about how this town will be.

Nonetheless, people come in and introduce themselves. I could share their names all at once but it would be a mess and I could never ask you to remember them all.

It is better to share the manners that I handle meeting them or rather what they do to help me at some point. It might sound a bit selfish but it is a bit easier.

And I would never want to overload you, dear reader.

But I meet a decent dose of people and the sheriff talks them into helping me out with furniture. Turns out some of them have items they are willing to part with to help me out.

It almost feels like a loan.

"I don't want you guys to worry about helping me out."

"Nonsense," Nina, a 39-year-old baker for the town--known for her endless bouts of fruit bread that she keeps fresh and tries to make various kinds every week that people seem to swarm to like piranhas to blood-- replies. "This is what we do. Besides, most of us have been on the verge of hoarding our old furniture more than we should. Besides, it would be better to part with it to help another out, then it would be tossed to the roadside for someone to pick up."

She makes a fair point.

I sit back with a chair provided by the sheriff himself and watch as people run in and out of my new residence. New to me, but not new to be built. It is far from freshly built.

I suspect it could use an upgrade or some repairs but that could happen another time.

Everyone brings in their furniture, working together rather than watching one another struggle to get something heavy or large into the house.

I have never been so grateful in my life. I'm humble, if nothing else, and wish I could do something in response to thank them other than common words.

It is a shame and maybe sometime I will come up with something. But for now, all I can offer them is words.

Once they are done, I thank them only to be welcomed to town in response. It is a charming response nonetheless.

I might have to partake of Nina's fruit bread sometime.

By the time all is said and done, I look around at the freshly furnished house.

This place looks like it has been set to sell.

You know what I mean...set up like a model house.

I appreciate that.

I get to the fridge and look in shock. Not only has furniture been brought in, but they have also stocked my fridge.

I find this odd coming from a town where people would rather raid your fridge before they would ever help you out.

Many people were cold back in Everett. But that was that town for sure.

A town with too many problems and not enough solutions. Too many people are eager to start things but very few will bother to care roughly to finish it without wasting time.

Most would rather distract and delay the inevitable.

And it comes as no surprise to me.

I grab a simple meal and toss it in the microwave.

Amazing how simple things can carry someone such as myself more than anything else.

I devour it and savor the taste. The flavors. It is nice to eat what is as close to a home-cooked meal as I'm going to get.

I hear ringing and it throws me off.

When did that happen?

When did someone install a home phone?

Well hell.

Guess I need to pay attention to details a bit more.

Maybe I'm thrown off. Maybe I'm still getting used to this town and the things they have done for me.

Or maybe I'm getting distracted.

That could be the case.

I take the time to check and find out the internet has been set up with a small card that has the information I need.

Wow.

The more I notice, the more I feel humbled and grateful.

There is something up about this town.

5

A hefty knock comes to the door and I squirm like I've been caught doing something wrong.

Why do I do that?

What am I expecting?

"You look a bit shaken," the sheriff says as I open the door.

"Just not used to people yet in this town," I reply.

"Fair enough."

"What can I do for you?"

"You are keen for details," he says.

"Excuse me?"

"I just meant you are good with spotting them I'm sure."

"Where is this going?"

"I was wondering if you would be able to help me out."

"Don't you have deputies and patrolmen and such?"

"I do but I am curious about you."

"Then ask questions. Never bring the worst of assumptions to mind."

"I don't know what that last part means but hey, I'll bite."

"I'm talking about you giving the kind of line that makes one think you are about to ask for their help on a case."

"No, I've got that covered. But I am curious about you."

What is his deal?

"What is there to be curious about?"

"May I come in?"

I don't see why not. "Sure."

This guy is something else. The kind of person that would make your head spin sometimes. The kind of guy that would make you wonder what goes through his mind.

It is clear he is more than just a wall of muscle. He is an enigma. I would inquire about him with the people in the town but I suspect that would only make them believe things like, "oh you must have a crush" or "he is a good guy; I don't see why you want to know."

It would set up so many flags it would be questionable to do at least.

I would have a better chance of learning about him from him than I would from asking others.

Conjecture only gets someone so far before it becomes baseless and pointless.

And some part of me would be remiss if I didn't mention the idea. It would make me suspicious as ever to ask about him but do nothing about it.

You know small towns: they could seem great on the outside but beneath the surface, there could be gossip paths and secrets that could tear anyone from their spot in moments.

Words are vile things. Sometimes they can be lethal. Other times, they are just sounds made from wagging one's tongue.

"What do you think of our town?" He goes from curious about me to want to know what I think of the town? That's a quick turn of events.

"I think it is something. The phrase smothering is the first. God help me. It's nothing against y'all but I'm not used to it. I'm not used to caring people and people so commanding at the same time. And somehow being accused of comes with no proof of why it could be a foundation."

He looks at me with some degree of confusion, curiosity, and hurt at the same time. I cannot hold back what I need to say when it happens.

6

He stays for something of an hour powdering me with questions and hoping I'll do his work for him which I tell him no. Then he leaves.

I don't know how to feel. I feel like he is more invested in me than his work. And that is a deep sadness to me.

As someone who wishes he could've been hired in 8 years of applying for work, I wish more would invest in their work. I wish more would go for what they enjoy rather than chasing a paycheck.

I wish more for a lot of people. But it doesn't work that way. No one goes into work they don't enjoy simply chasing a paycheck as a means to survive in the world.

And those that wanted that work and didn't get that work, are denied it because someone else gets it.

Another that bothers me in the realm of employ is this: too many places hire those they want rather than those that are starving for work and need the work. Friends should not be quickly hired for employment as they would make strange bedfellows.

Or maybe I have a proverbial stick up my own ass and wish nothing more than for society to be better. C'est la vie.

The right can never happen without a heavy push and the wrong will always happen out of convenience.

That night I'm curled up in a recliner because my lazy ass doesn't want to leave the living space. No tv but that's fine.

Fuck all know this town is cold at night. It's a shame I don't want to move. It's all good.

When I get comfortable, I listen to the sound of silence. It's almost deafening.

I hate it. Everything about it has become vile.

Morning comes and I need coffee. All the coffee. I need it. The sun is being a spot of hell in the sky and as I climb out of the chair, I hiss at the light as I stretch and pop my joints. Fuck it to hell, it hurts right off the bat.

I am not sleeping in that damn thing tonight. That's for sure.

Just as I toss on a robe and start for the kitchen, there is a heavy knock to the door.

Based on the deep base and starting crack to the door—I can basically see the splinters beginning—I suspect it is the sheriff.

Come to bother me once more. I groan and make my way. The heavy meaty hand hits the door thrice more for another two sets before I get to it.

Such an annoyance this impatience in the morning. Curse the fool that beats at a door of an unawakened being.

A person like myself without coffee makes for a deeply angry adversary but that doesn't stop people from doing it.

I open the door and find it to be none other than him.

"Well howdy."

I groan at him looking like someone that had recently faced a bucket or wet tee shirt challenge with great disdain. "What…" I groan.

"Not a morning person. Got it," he says and I groan again. "Would it help if I brought coffee? I got four kids because I didn't know what you drank," he says.

He is trying to be decent. I get that. But merciful people above, I hate this more than ever.

I grab the container and uncap the lids and sip each one.

With a grimace and an unfortunate love for the caffeine nectar of nature, I start sipping at one and out the others in the fridge for possible later use.

I don't tell him but I suspect he knows of my thanks and secret addiction.

7

"So what do you want?" I ask downing the second coffee.

"I could use help."

"What is there to help you with? I have no history. No priors. No degree. No work. What the hell could I end up doing that would work well for you?"

"I could use someone that has a sharp eye."

"Then befriend a silent one or a sharpshooter," I remark.

A joke that is wasted time on him. I should hang out with him or get to know his tastes first.

Or maybe he could grow a sense of humor. "What are you talking about?" He asks.

See? Wasted.

"Don't worry about it. Do yourself a favor and find someone more qualified."

"Everyone rose does something. You are the only one not working."

Rude!

"And what if I do online work? What would you say then?"

"Do you do online work?" Aside from blogging about the random musings in my mind, that tends to net me small digits give or take every month.... nope, but he doesn't onto that.

Yet I cannot tell lies. I am nothing if not honest.

"I do not."

"Come with me."

Guess I don't have a choice. What a surprise.

He drags me to the office after he lets me get changed—how quaint—and I look around. The whole thing is one room. That's it.

A counter with a coffee pot or two and Styrofoam cups. He seems to keep it simple. Kudos to him.

I fight the urge to have what could be a crappy cup of coffee.

"So what do you expect me to do?" I ask.

He looks at me and looks at the typewriter.

"I want you to type out what you remember of the scene. Share whatever you want but put it down on the page. This isn't school so there is no grade."

"One thing first," I state.

"What is your name?"

"It's Charlie."

I sit down and curl my wrists just right so I don't end up getting the early stages of carpal tunnel. Curse my need to crack my knuckles.

I cannot help it. I just want to feel no pain as minimal pain in my joints as I can and given the glares and lectures my doctor gives me, a part of me doesn't give a shit.

When I get done, he looks at me. "Damn," he says.

He looks at the small stack of 2 pages. I don't know if that counts as a stack but you get the idea.

Meanwhile, I watch as he takes the pages, sleeves them up, and reads through them like an editor.

Nerves get the best of me. As if he is judging me. As if he is going to give me a grade or degrade me or something.

I am not sure.

Why is he treating what I cranked down as delicate as evidence?

Wait...is it evidence? Is he using it against me? Is he using me?

I feel myself beginning to shut down. A need to protect me. I don't want to get close to or wracked to anyone but this town has a strange effect on people.

"Do you need anything else?" I ask.

"Your number," he says hourly.

"Excuse me?" I am taken aback. I don't know if he is being honest or flirting but I am not for it. I won't let anyone get close to me.

I don't want it and I don't need that pressure. That's way too much for me.

"To call you in case I need more."

I eye him oddly. I don't like that turn of phrase. I am not wild on the idea of having to do a lot of things.

"You set the damn thing up. Don't lie to me. You have it," I say and head out before he can get a word in edgewise. I don't want to think of what more could happen.

I already had odd dreams of the corpse and what could've been. Or at least the many situations that could've gone down. Either way, I brush it from my mind and make my way home.

Once home after stopping at the bakery—what could I say; I'd heard she had more products to try and she seemed to find a taste tester in me—I put the stuff up.

What can I say? Coffee is a comfort for me. Not just an energy provider.

8

I couldn't sleep. Thoughts of why Charlie seemed focus led on me and fixated bothered me.

I don't know why. I don't know what his issue is but it's something.

Morning comes far too quickly for me and I'm downing day-old coffee like it's fresh because interestingly enough: it still is.

What are they putting in the coffee around here? Damn.

Getting the place cleaned up, I hear a knock to the door and suspect it to be Charlie. His being enamored with me is a tad worrisome.

I don't want to seem harsh but I also don't want to be coddled and hovered over like a child being smothered by a controlling parent. The idea of life is supposed to be making your own choices not being dictated.

When I get to the door, I find there is no one there but 3 bags are waiting for me.

I'm hesitant. Should I call Charlie despite?

Would he find it odd for me to call him about this?

I suspect he might laugh at me.

I give in.

I am quick to dial him as he leaves the card on the phone.

"Yes?" He asks.

"Is it normal to have three bags randomly delivered to your porch?" I ask.

"Did you order anything?"

"I did not."

"I'm on my way, " he says and hangs up on me.

Guess I ought to start laundry and become presentable huh?

When he makes it to my place, I have not moved the bags but I have deposited a load of laundry into the wash.

I sip at my own fresh tea that I've made with items people have chosen to grace me with. I am quite grateful even if most were complete strangers and still are.

"I see you followed my advice, " he says.

"Of course. I'm not a simpleton. I'm a follower of a trusting word."

He blushes. "You trust me?"

"Until you give me a reason not to, yes," I reply.

He gives me a curious look. "Well, that is a moment ruined."

"What moment?" I ask.

He looks at me then back to the bags. "What?"

"I said what moment?"

He is stunned in silence but chooses to ignore my question. He grabs a pair of tweezers and proceeds to pick out the items in each bag one after another, quickly snapping a photograph of each one on his camera phone.

He may be odd but you have got to admire his skills and precision. The way he handles a phone reminds me of teenagers that used to walk by the house.

Reminds me that oddly, I still hate that I lost my job as a reviewer of books and shows and some games because of my parents' deaths.

It is what it is.

I've moved on.

When he is done, he looks at me. "Looks like I need your skills again, " he sighs.

"Why?"

He taps on each bag twice in a signal to have me look into each of the bags.

I glance at each one without touching them.

Lovely. Perfect! Body parts. A head and two arms. Where is the rest I wonder?

I notice a note stapled to an arm.

I point it out to him.

33

He grabs it carefully and snaps a picture of it before glancing at it.

"A whole being is the sum of its parts. I wonder if maybe this being was ever whole," it reads.

Why does this seem very religious and occult like?

I wonder so much.

I cannot begin to fathom this.

"Something tells me this is going to get worse," I remark.

"I would say so, " he says. He puts the items back in and gathers the bags into his car. A car that is in desperate need of a cleaning. Amazing how the outside looked clean and pristine but the inside looked worse for wear.

How long has he been sheriff?

9

"Do you even have a coroner or an examiner or coroner in this town?" I ask.

"We have an examiner, yes," he says.

"You might want to take that to them."

"I'll call Eddie, " he says and dials his phone. He is quick about it.

"Who is Eddie?" I ask.

"He brought the bed and the coffee pot," he replies.

I suddenly feel like I never want to sleep in a bed or use a coffee pot. "When you brought over coffee, where did you get it from?"

"Caffeine Cathy's by the book shop, " he replies.

I make a note to visit it. Or at least to find some way to make some income and visit it and the book shop.

Sweet cripes. A bookstore? Where has it been all my life? I know one thing above all: I don't plan on visiting the mystery section. That's for damn sure.

"How long have you been sheriff?" I ask.

"A long time." Talk about tension with a T.

"Okay smartass. When did you become a sheriff?"

"When the last one died, " he replies.

Talk about vague as hell. I'm getting nowhere. How did this asshat become a sheriff?

He is gone after a moment of awkward bullshittery.

And I'm glad for it. As I make my way out of the house, I am precocious and a bit paranoid. I rush off to the town setting itself.

Once these, I look for work and find nothing available.

This sucks. What's a guy got to do to get some work around here? I mean come on.

Doesn't matter. Looks like back to online work for me.

I get back to the house and start looking on my phone.

Nothing around.

Dammit. What is the deal around here?

Something has to give. I refuse to be that person that gives in and has to solve crimes.

I won't be that nosy person that eavesdrops. I just won't.

"I never got your name, " Charlie says and I jump nearly out of my skin. Things are a bit rough for me.

"Bill," I remark.

"Another simple name." It is a common name. I'm sure there are at least 20 thousand Bills in the world.

None of it would surprise me. It is what it is as far as I am concerned.

"What are you doing here?" I ask.

"I came offering coffee and a job for you."

"Doing what? Your job?"

"If you wanted to help me with my job all you had to do was ask," he smirks.

I laugh. "Yeah, I'm good. I'll find work on my own."

"I know you were job hunting recently." Cripes. Is the man stalking me? Or are people being his spies from the shadows?

"What does that have to do with you?" Yeah, I prefer my craziness with my bread. Not from a sheriff of all people. But most sheriffs tend to be a little off their rocker way some point.

Note to self: make crazy bread. It can be therapeutic for me.

God knows I haven't baked in a while. Might be time to get back to it. I just won't make a business of it. It will be just for me.

That's the way I kind of want my life to be. For me. No one else. No shame in being happy being alone after all.

At least then the only person you can hurt is yourself and even then, it is never with the best of intentions.

"So what would you have me doing since you are being so open for offering me work?" I am curious where he is going to take this. I really am.

He seems to want to know so much about me it is a bit creepy. Almost like he is a stalker. Don't get me wrong. I'm not out to find faults in people. I just don't trust strangers for this reason.

This particular attitude and air about them are very unsettling, to say the least. I don't know if I like it. But I am the fool that bought the house. It seems I don't have much choice now. Especially with no money coming in to save up and use later to my advantage.

"I want you to observe the scenes and memorize them."

Wait. "I have to stop you already."

"Why?"

"First off, this will not do you anyway or in a court of law. And second, given that I am a witness to these things it would greatly screw you over."

"I'm not saying for this case, " he says, pinching the bridge of his nose in frustration.

"Fine then. Seems I have no option."

"I don't like the way you said that, " he says.

"And I don't like this eerie stalker-like mentality this town has going on but one in one hand, shit in the other, " I remark in just as much frustration.

"We are not stalking you. We are just close-knit and to be honest, you are the newest event to happen to us."

Oh no he didn't.

"Event?" I ask as I begin to glare. "I'm not some carnival, fair, or party. I'm just a person. Someone that wants to live his life. To blend in and not stand out. So if I were you, it would refrain from calling anyone an event."

He looks wounded and while I feel like a complete ass, I am glad to put it out there. I don't mind people getting to know me but use conventional manners of doing so. Conversate, talk to someone for fucks sake. Don't stalk and stare.

This isn't a horror movie or anything. Geez.

"Look I'm sorry."
"Get out."
"But..."
"Just go."

With that, he walks out, closing the door gently behind him.

10

The next few days are quiet as I sit back at the house. I must admit my curiosity gets the best of me as I find myself thinking about the body parts.

Who did they belong to? What is the deal with Charlie being so off and snippy? I cannot deny the feeling that he knew them. But given how small this town is, wouldn't everyone be acting like this? Or is he just the person that is open about his feelings compared to those that choose to hide like recluses in this town?

I have many questions and I'm sure there will be no answers to them. Maybe in time, I will.

For now, I know little to nothing. I'm also curious about the justice system. Is it a court trial? Or is it capture and send someone away sort of thing?

I have much to learn about this town and it feels like not enough time to learn it. I suspect I won't be in this town for long. And I don't know why I have this peculiar feeling.

Something feels amiss. Something seems off.

When I see him again, he is at my doorway with a small bag of donuts and coffee.

5 coffees. Either he is sucking up big time or he got me four coffees and himself one.

Either way, I feel compelled to let him in, so I do so.

He comes in and closes the door with a nudge of his shoe. I don't mind it. At least he doesn't slam it like a neanderthal. That would be a screw you.

"I come bringing news and tithes. Which do you want first?"

He is not playing fair. It seems he knows I feed off curiosity despite not wanting to work for him. I cannot deny what seems to consume my mind and soul. My body just wants donuts. Go figure. Me a glutton for gluten.

When he sets the bag down and reveals sweet pastries of all sorts, my eyes and face betray me. I almost glow at the sight of such delectable darlings. They speak to me like a siren's song.

Charlie doesn't play fair.

But I know he has news and if I request the news while eating, I'm liable to lose appetite. So I better wait and hear the news first. Except for coffee. Nothing shall stop me from having that.

"Bring on the news first, " I say, snatching and sipping a coffee. He grabs his and proceeds.

"So the head and arms belonged to the first victim's wife. Shame really. We embrace LGBT plus couples in this town and deny those that have too small a mind."

Too small? What is just small enough for their bullshit?

"Too small? What is the right kind of small mind?"

"Every brand of small mind is one to watch out for! Ours just happens to be precautious and caring at the same time."

Odd combo one would say. But it is bound to happen. I just wonder if I am too quick to embrace or too quick to judge.

"So what does all this have to do with me?" I ask.

"I am starting to believe you are a victim of circumstances. Wrong place wrong time kind of thing."

Odd. "I'm not so sure people have been seeing me that way."

"Relax. No one thinks you did it. Everyone more or less pities that it is happening to you more than anything."

So I am the source of a pity party. Lovely. Not what I would call comforting by any means. I wish I could use it to my advantage and get some work but that doesn't seem to be the case.

It is what it is. I might fire up a book review site or something. Start with a social media page and account. Grow from there. I just wonder how to get the word out about it. Can I post something? Or will it just come naturally? Should I start with what I have in my possession? Or should I figure out something else? I haven't a clue.

Maybe I'll start with the classics that I have in possession. Even if they have been reviewed hundreds of times by others.

It would be something. A start or two. A way to pick up some traffic.

Who knows?

11

I spend the majority of the day reading a book I've read plenty of times.

When I am done, I review it on my phone, and once done editing, I hit the post button for it and disappear into another book. I get through a second one when he bursts into my home.

"Can I help you?" I ask above my reading glasses. "How are you?"

"I'm alive and here. Why?"

"Just asking. I need your help."

Of course, he does. He only comes to see me when he wants something. Don't get me wrong. I know that is how some towns are and how some people are but it is almost ridiculous. It begins to become people using people. No appreciation just using each other. That's not how the community is. That shouldn't be how a sense of community is. What is wrong with people?

It is pathetic. Ridiculous even. But it doesn't matter to the simple idiots that live here.

I swear there is something more going on. Someone just isn't being really seen. They are seen by not truly seen and it is sad that I notice that before someone else does.

"What with?"

"Can you come with me?"

Of course. Seems that I don't get to do what I want. Wow, that sounds selfish and for a second, I hate myself for thinking that let alone wanting to say it.

"Fine."

I am quick to type a review while I'm in the car with him. I wonder where he is taking me and what I am going to be in for in the first place.

I guess I'm going to find out in some form or another.

When we get there, I have already posted the review. This place is different. "What is going on?" I ask when I see a cluster of people waiting for us.

"This is a welcome to the community and town kind of thing. Everyone felt like they wanted to welcome you properly."

Not going to lie, I'm a little uncomfortable. I'm the kind of person that wishes to suffer in silence but it seems that won't happen.

Three and a half hours later, I am so partied out and full and comforted by the town, I am eager to get some rest. I might crash by reading another book.

Turns out some of them have been checking out my blog reviews already. And the bookstore owner Terry has told me if I ever need books to let them know so I can come in and check out their selection. It might have slipped at one point that I didn't have income happening yet. There came an agreement out of it.

Terry is full of surprises. Didn't think I was talking to an amazing decent person but hey, you can learn a lot from a simple conversation. Especially when deals are struck.

Terry takes the time to drive me home and ask me questions. Nothing intrusive by any means but common and decent ones most people ask.

12

A week passes and I suspect something is up. I have been reading so much I'm sure my brain can turn a page before my frigging fingers bother to. A serious case of telepathy going on and stupidity quickly following it.

No one comes breaking into the house. No drama. This is odd. I'm not sure.

I don't know what's up but something is. Basically two weeks of no death? No bodies? Odd. Very odd. Either a killer is giving up or they are planning. And that sends warning bells off in my head.

When I get done with the books I have, I make a note to go to the book shop and get new ones. Ones that could make for fun reviews. I'm not a book snob nor am I someone that reads a single genre or two so it could be something.

As I'm heading out to grab some take out for dinner that night—at least I thought smart to tuck a small amount of money aside--I spot Charlie pulling up.

"Where are you off to?" He asks.

"Celebrating getting my books done and reviewed," I remark.

"Nice. Let me take you out."

"Why? I'm not dating you."

"Just let me do it."

"For that attitude, you are pulling, hell no. Now leave me be." I might be many things but I am not going to be submissive to this dickhead. No wonder he is alone.

With that, I keep walking and make my way to the taco bar. Once inside, I put in, pay, and quickly get my order before heading back home.

I don't mind small towns but this is ridiculous and Charlie's being obsessed and enamored with me to hell does him no favors at all.

He approaches me on the way back.

He looks at me once more wounded but he doesn't leave. What is his deal? There is no chance of love. Maybe friends if he keeps his distance and backs up but come on. I want nothing more.

"What is up with you?" He asks.

"Excuse me?"

"You move into the town. We welcome you and you keep people away? What's the deal with that?"

"Let me make this quite plain, " since he seems to not get it even when I have told him time and time again, "I come from a place where people only want to be close when they want something or if they want dirt on you. It was cute at first but it taught me a dark lesson.

Don't ever trust people fully. It only leads to you getting hurt, betrayed, or mocked. And I will have none of the above. Do you get it now?"

By now he has stopped his car and looked at me with such shock as if I have told him that Santa or otherwise is not real. As if I have crushed his every hope and dream.

And while I don't want to make enemies or break hearts, I would rather be left alone if at all possible. But it seems when one is in a small town, that idea goes to the shitter.

I guess I have no choice but to deal with it.

So much for peace, quiet, and solitude.
Hello, bullshit!

13

Another week comes and goes. I am here. Reading and eating. I'm sure I'm putting on weight but so what. Body image is in the eye of the beholder. Not fashion people. Dumb asses. Fuck those that feel being small and frail thin is the only way to be sexy.

When I get done with the new book, I review it and grab the mail after. I need to get some money coming in. I'm sure this town gives some lean but I don't want to lean on them too much.

For the hell of it, I check comments and such for my blog. Holy shit!

A few thousand people have seen it and some have donated to the page. I mean don't get me wrong. I know most people don't think about donating to blogs but damn. Cash donations or electronic ones matter just as equally. I check my card and my digital account.

$1,000.

All of which are accessible and usable on the card right away.

I check to see if I can pay with the account card.

Sure can.

Damn. I didn't expect people to want to pay attention to a classic and teen book blog.

Guess I know what I'll be doing for a while. I decide I want to buy a few books to celebrate. Books due to be destined for greatness among LGBT plus people.

Why not?

Most people don't give them or their work a damn chance. And it is pathetic. They are people too. As someone that sees everyone just as equals, it is only right for someone to help be a voice.

Even if I know next to nothing. Oh and rule of thumb for those that are nosy and want to know, I'm asexual. I'm content and good on my own. I don't need or want anyone to make me feel happy. I'm good on my own.

It was kind of odd for me to explain that to mom and dad. And now here I am.

When I get out the door once I'm done paying for the bills, I spot Charlie coming to see me.

What does he want now?

Is he coming to harass me? Use me? Make me do the dirty work for him?

Or has he found his decency and has learned how to be a human being again?

I guess I'm going to find out huh.

"What's the deal, Charlie?" I ask.

He looks at me oddly. Then he speaks. "Came to check on you. That's all, " he replies.

"I'm good."

"I saw your blog. Way to go on the flood of comments, " he says.

He knows of my blog? Wow. Damn. I didn't expect that.

He smirks as if knowing what I'm thinking. "Yeah, I know about it. I also know that it has been getting a lot of book sales for Terry. People have been flooding the classics and teen sections." Well then. I didn't expect it at all.

I guess I have a degree of influence after all. It continues to amaze me, the power of words. How one can express themselves without saying a word.

14

"Thank you, " I remark.

He nods. "Where are you off to?"

"I was going to get a sweet treat and a few new books if Terry's shop was open."

"It's open trust me, " he smiles. "Want a ride?"

"Thanks but I'm going to walk there."

He nods. "Mind if I join you?" While I would typically be frustrated, stressed, and more about this I have decided to take another route. "Sure."

He parks his car and gets out. We start walking side by side. Making our way into downtown with ease.

"How is the case going?" I ask.

"It's going. We've had two more bodies show up."

"Any relation to the first two?"

"Yeah. Either someone has it out for this person's entire social line or the family did wrong somehow."

"Why do you say that?" What can I say? I'm curious.

"Refresh my mind, are you quick to get queasy?"

I shake my head. "It takes a lot to get my queasy."

53

He whips out his phone. He pulls up 2 pictures and shows each one to me.

I glance at each one, looking at the details. "Maybe it is my detailed eye but I see a pattern. A few similarities."

"Exactly. There seems to be a pattern for sure."

I mean it makes sense. Both patterns show similar slash marks, not to mention the marks around the wrists. Seems very pattern-based to me. But hey, I'm not someone to admire dark marks or anything of the sort. I am his tone with a self-trained detailed set of eyes. I don't know why I trained myself for it why I trained myself to do it but I figure sooner or later it will come in handy. And it seems to be helping Charlie so I guess it is something.

It is making some use of it.

"You know I do appreciate your help. Even if I cannot tell you many thanks to you being a witness."

It's funny. I've never been a fan of mysteries. I couldn't handle it because to me unless they were borderline thrillers, they never quite intrigued me. And yet here I am, basically the outsider that I'd helped solve through observation yet not getting to be a part of it all.

This sucks royally. If I could help, I would only help with the observation. A sort of surveyor or manners and situation.

And this is going to have to be the best I can. The joy thing I can do is give insight with nosiness.

It is what it is.

15

We continue to talk as we make our way to the bookshop. I decide to switch it up and head to the bakery first. I grab a slice of cheesecake and he gets a few slices of banana bread and zucchini bread. When we are done, I head out and to the bookshop.

Charlie says he has a few things to do and parts ways with me. I do appreciate that he dotes on me and it is fair that he is keeping me up to date on the case.

I still hate that I am not more active in it but it is what it is. I know it is a matter of time.

I get to the bookshop and my eyes got huge. Sweet gods. This place is amazing. To organize and the shelves are low enough to look over it. Book worms could observe each other or maybe end up meeting and getting together with this kind of thing.

I head to the clearly marked sections of classics, and teens. I look around and grab a small handbasket.

I grab a few books that I've been meaning to read in the classics section. The more I grab, the more I wonder if I am going too far or grabbing too much.

Amazing how the size of classics varies. Some are small enough to be used for a tissue while others look like the ultimate tome from hell.

Lucky for me, I've already read Moby Dick. Gods above know that is one book that could drag on if you aren't focused somehow.

And something to know about me, I tend to get lost in something and ignore surroundings when I'm focused.

Not that it is something fundamental about me in the first place.

I grab a few others and take the time to make my way to the teen section. Odd for a man of 20 something to be perusing a young adult section but it is what it is.

And at least there is a degree of variety. As I'm grabbing some teen books that are marked with a rainbow thanks to the use of a bookmark sticking out of them, Terry comes around the corner.

"Hey! Glad you could make it. Don't worry about paying for books. Just keep up the good work with the blog. I'm sure it will work wonders."

I don't know about that. "Do you do any advertising?" I ask.

"I do what I can. The town seems to love coming here and that works for me," they reply.

"Why don't you do some online advertising? It might be something to help out."

"Tell you what, I have an idea."

"What's that?" I ask, grabbing another half dozen young adult books.

"You mention that you got the books from the shop, and we can call it even. The books are free for you and you alone. Please don't mention that part."

That is a bit of common sense. I don't mind it. I won't mention it because that would be bad for business. That would only come back to bite us both in the ass.

"I promise to keep that part between us." We both laugh.

They wait for me to finish grabbing a decent amount before bagging up the books for me to take home.

I'm excited. I'm a bookworm like that.

And you better believe, I'm going to take a photo of that.

But damn.

I need to get a new phone. Or something. A computer that isn't rustic as sin would be nice but it is a matter of time.

Being smart. Being patient and pinching pennies.

I need something good going on.

The next few days are spent reading and dealing with Charlie checking on me like an older parent.

Or an older sibling for that matter. It is what it is. Charlie continues to break the rules for me and I don't know why. I just know it is true. I know it is what it is.

Aside from that, I'm busy with reading.

By the time I choose to take a break, I don't want to look at pages but it doesn't seem like that will be the case.

When you spend your days reading and writing reviews, sometimes you need to see the world.

Even if you start to see what could be seen as "plot holes" in the real world aka the flaws.

I think if I could, I would rather live in the pages of a book. Even if it is a horror novel. It would seem anything but dull and it would keep me more than busy.

I step outside and breathe in some air. It is nice.

And that is when I spot it: another fucking body part on my fence. Not only this but they have taken down part of the fence--the corpse in question.

Son of a bitch!

Here we go.

This is where it always gets interesting.

Charlie knocks on the door--the guy has a signature knock guy, what more can I say?--and I call for him to come around back.

"What's up? How are you...oh. Really? Back to go? No collecting? None of that?"

Lame he is being with the monopoly references but I get what he means. This is back where it started.

"Son of a bitch! Let me get some bags and make a call."

"What the hell am I going to do? Tell me that," I remark rhetorically.

He shrugs. "Fair."

With that, he heads out of the back gate and makes his way to the car. I just sit there leaning on the wall to the porch. It is what it is.

Frankly, sometimes you just have to have a sense of humor about it.

And as much as I love to try and be real, it seems to be a drag for some. So I'll be blunt. I'll have a degree of fun and go from there.

16

Five hours. That's how long it took. I ended up sitting up on the front porch for five hours.

Turns out recently, Charlie has hired some officers that have come around. Don't get me wrong, I have waited for it to be a thing. I just wonder what more could come of it.

I try to avoid reading more but given that I am dealing with this and need something to do other than fumbling with my damn phone.

I start to open up the book when another junior cop comes over and drills me with the same questions over and over again.

Sweet god.

Someone give this bastard a chill pill or something.

He is going to piss me off.

And that is the last thing anyone should want to do to a witness or a victim.

I know what he is trying to do. Trying to trip me up.

And sadly Charlie is doing nothing about it.

The man is the sheriff and he is acting beneath his employees. He is acting like they run the show.

This is pathetic.

Charlie speaks up after it happens for the 4th time. They can try all they want. You can't bullshit what you see. That's for sure.

Especially with the number of bodies that I've seen.

And with my sharp mind, it doesn't surprise. Most people seem to think if you repeat questions enough, someone smart will slip up and misspeak or fumble their answers.

That's not the case. It just pisses us off.

But I'm not one to brag about my intelligence.

When all is said and done, they are gone and Charlie looks at me with worry. "You aren't going to hold their attitudes against me, are you?" He asks.

"Why the hell would I do that?" I don't know what his mindset is but I'm sure I will find out at some point or another.

"I don't know. I feel like you would be that person that does that."

Ouch. So he pegs me for being shallow. I don't appreciate that.

"I don't know whether to be worried or upset that you let me do that."

"Look I don't want to upset you."

Too damn late. "What about me makes you think that?" My voice is ringing with hurt and a hint of fury.

I don't want to be this transparent but damn if he doesn't make me into this person. I don't want to let my trust be on my sleeve but damn. He is starting to make me want to give up on people. To stop giving people the benefit of the doubt.

"I don't know. You tend to stick to being secluded rather than chatting and mingling with people."

Why in fresh hell is that a bad thing?

"So let me wrap my head around this. I've been to a small town for a short time and I'm just supposed to let people walk all over me. I'm supposed to be one of those idiots that wants to know everything and everyone like a damn Hallmark movie."

"I didn't say that."

"No, but for a sheriff that is trying to be a decent human being and be open, you suck at it. Being told that I brush people off is a bad thing is a very sneaky way of saying I need to share my life story to everyone that I meet and that I need to pretend to be someone I'm not."

"I am not trying to."

"Then what is it? Is it because I'm a bit paranoid after having 2 corpses now 3 at my new house? Or is it that I'm still somehow mourning the deaths of my parents and having been forced out in a short time? Tell me, what part of myself makes me the bad guy. I really want to know." I might be getting a little overzealous about this but this is my life and Charlie seems to think it is okay to expect someone to be someone they are not.

This is not a typical movie or show or whatever. This is my life. If I don't find a reason to trust you, I'm not going to trust you.

It should be that simple. And until you can prove you are trustworthy otherwise, there will be a conflict unspoken between us.

I figured that would be common sense. But clearly, I'm *wrong*.

Or maybe some people fucked up in the head to expect someone to be so forthcoming about everything from the get-go.

Here's a secret from me to you: most people if not all have secrets. Everyone has to feel a sense of comfort and safety and trust in order to want to divulge it. Some secrets are painful and don't ever want to be shared. It is the nature of being a fucking secret.

"Look, this is getting too heated."

"It is. You do what you have to do sheriff. I have to do what I have to do. You don't have to always check on me. My wellbeing is fine. I'll call you if I want to chat with you. I'll call you or text you if I find another body. In the meantime, you live your life and I'll live mine. Is that okay with you?"

He nods. "It is."

"Then have a good one."

With that, I head into the house and shut the door behind me. I'm seething with internal rage and start to calm down as I am shaking from frustration.

Now I understand the frustration that Lady Catherine felt to a slight degree in *Pride and Prejudice*.

The nerve of some people.

16

    I take some medicine for the headache that has come to lash at my brain so fiendishly. I sit back after grabbing a small pint of ice cream and devour it with quick succession. I don't bother to worry about how it would look or how I would look after the fact.

    I curl up in the recliner and fall asleep. It will not do wonders for my back in a good manner but at least I could get a degree of sleep.

    That much I'm sure of.

    This is one of those times I miss my parents. I miss the father's comforting words and a mother's sense of touch. I miss the shit I went through in my hometown. Even if it was vile to the core. At least I knew how to cope with it.

    I knew how to handle a lot of things. As for here, Basin is a whole other town. A town of a lot of deep-rooted things and issues and families that I know nothing about but I suspect I will be facing at some point or another.

    I'm not sure I could be cut out for this town.

    But I know I don't have the means to go bouncing around. Sometimes the best way to deal with your issues is to face them head-on. I did it when I was told I had two weeks to get a place and get out.

    I did it when I first dealt with a body in my new house's backyard. I will find out what the deal is around here and I will face it.

    The next day, I slip into Nina's bakery and put in an order for some of the fresh bread, a bag of cinnamon rolls, and a few muffins. I head out and stop at the coffee shop before heading back.

    I'm slowly mustering my sense of direction with this town as I make my way around in the car I've got.

    It is not that big at all. This town is very much so that I firmly believe I could walk from one end to the other and back in maybe an hour's time.

    Interesting that I'm just now figuring this out. Especially when I have walked around it and to certain spaces a time or two.

    It is as I get back home that I watch the sky become clouded and rain begins to come down in sheets.

    Odd.

    I don't remember getting a weather alert from the town's weather broadcast.

    As if on cue, my phone goes off alerting me to the rain. I get inside and put most items away. I've downed a coffee and a few muffins--two banana nut and a zucchini muffin--so I feel a bit energized.

I might even start working out. Oh, who am I kidding? I've got a love affair with a recliner and books that could never be ended.

I wouldn't mess with the natural order of my life. That would be absurd.

I make my way to the porch with a book I've been reading on and sit back in a shitty chair that I've bought on my phone in the past few days. I just found it delivered early this morning.

I sit back and get used to sitting in it.

At the same time, I dive back into the book. To hell with the world. I don't mind losing myself in a book.

It is a matter of time.

I know what it comes down to at this point: disappearing into something and letting the day melt away.

The day seems to melt away from me. And I don't mind it. The sound of rain becomes rather comforting. I don't get up much other than to use the bathroom and get a replacement drink. I don't bother to eat because I don't want to ruin the sanctity of the book. The condition of the book matters to someone like myself.

It is like respecting the time and the hard work that the author put into it. It is a sign that you enjoyed it or you didn't enjoy it.

I can understand finger oils and such but when one drops a stain on it or something, I don't know. It sort of pisses me off.

Maybe I'm too snobby about it.

That could be the case.

A few days come and go. The weather changes to bright and cheery and a part of me hates it during the mornings. I'm not a morning person. Go figure.

I sip at my coffee--I have a decent relationship with a delivery person that is saving up or their transition. To which I say good for them. I give a decent tip and I spend a lot of time reading and reviewing. Might as well make the most of it.

God knows the blog seems to be taking off and that surprises me.

I don't know what it is. Maybe I am simple and to the point with it. I'm dropping maybe a paragraph at most talking about what I like while being vague but hey. It is what it is.

And the tips seem to be coming in drastically which surprises me. I don't know what it is. I just know it is happening.

17

I figure I could take a week off to do something. Bond with others, figure things out, something. I could use the time of reading and write for a review. It is something good for me.

It is a matter of time. I just have to have fun.

The question is: what could I do?

Then I remember the falls that are just outside of town. The weather has been nice.

Something tells me I might run into Charlie there. I don't know what it is. Call it my intuition.

I don't know if I want to do it. I would be lying if I said I wasn't hesitant about it. I don't want to run into Charlie because he seems to be my curse. Every time I am near him or have spent any degree of time with him, something seems to come out of it.

Something bad. Bodies dropping and more. I feel like something is going on in that department.

It is what it is.

I won't go to the waterfall. No matter how much of paradise it will be. I'll just sit back and hang out. Maybe take some walks around town. Maybe walk around the woods that surround the town on one side and consider hiking up the hills on the other side.

I get out the door and take in the temperature. It is bright as for sin out there but at the same time, it is cool. How does that work?

I suspect it has to do with elevation and the hills and the woods. This town is what it is.

It is never going to not surprise me. It is never going to be normal. Always going to be odd.

I am going to make the most of it because why the hell not. It is strangely becoming comforting, the discourse of this town.

I change clothes to be comfortable and walk around town.

I figure I could use the time to myself. I don't want to spend any more major money than I have. Things have been steadying out and I don't want to run out of funds before bills come around.

Come on. You know what I'm talking about. Money tends to become tight around bill paying time.

I might grab a snack and a drink if anything. But we will see.

It is kind of nice to take this walk around. To observe people in their natural routines.

It is as I am heading into Nina's bakery that I run into Charlie...again.

He has been driving around, trying to be nonchalant. There is no doubt in my mind he is not subtle. He is not that great at blending in.

A 39-year-old beefcake blending in this small town? As if.

Especially with how people manage to stare at him like he is a slice of cake.

Again, not my taste. I'm good. Don't get me wrong, I know what sex could be like and I know what I need so I tend to it. But I don't bother to find that one person.

I'm good without that person. I'm good on my own. It works for me and I'm more comfortable this way.

But I digress.

I get inside despite wanting to avoid running into him and order some croissants. 3 to be exact with a spread of various jams and a sweet tea.

She nods and smiles at me, Nina before I pay for it.

"I hope you are doing well. What you have been dealing with around here is nothing short of awful," she says when she brings the items to my table a few moments later.

"I'm making do."

"Mind if I sit for a moment?"

"Help yourself." It would be rude as hell if I told her to get back to work and fuck off. She has likely been on her feet for hours and could use a break. I don't remember seeing a stool or anything anywhere behind the counter so her dogs have to be barking.

I bite into the smooth perfection that is the first croissant with pumpkin jam. It is amazing, as per usual.

I savor the taste of it with each chew and bite.

"I'm sorry if this is too far but are you okay? You seem distracted," she says.

I sip at the tea to help down the food and take a moment before responding.

"I'm a little rough for wear but I'm using the book reading and reviewing to help me get through it all."

She looks at me with concern. "Are you taking breaks?" She puts a hand on my free one.

"I am taking this week off. I figured a nice walk and some air would be good. A bit of time for me to be me."

"If you ever want to hang out with someone, let me know. We can hang out and chat in here if you want," she says. She nods her head to behind the counter.

I nod. "I appreciate that." I dive into the second croissant.

18

I get back to the walk and embrace the town for what it is. At least I try to.

I have fresh tea with me in hand and make my way around. People are stuck in this sad case of routine.

I don't want to be that person. I don't want to be that person that falls into it. Sadly I have been developing a routine without meaning to.

It is what it is.

That is basic life right there. Routine. The same shit, day in and day out.

It is sad but it is true at the same time.

My mind jumps back to the case. What is going on with it? What about it?

As if he knows what is going on in my head at all times, Charlie pulls up to the house.

"I figured I could update you on the case," he says.

I sigh which can be far too revealing. Too indicative of what is going on in my head. "What is going on?"

"We are waiting for another strike."

Is he serious? This is what it comes down to? A waiting game?

When 4 people have been cut down, it shouldn't come down to another strike for something to be done. Run some evidence. Do something other than sitting on your ass sipping coffee. Do something for fuck's sake.

"And what good would another dead body do? You aren't testing evidence. When was the last time you lifted a fingerprint?"

He knows I am right which is why he has a guilty look on his face.

"I'm afraid there is nothing else we can do."

That is a crock of crap.

I decided to slightly change the subject.

"So how is the crew working out?"

"It's not. I don't put up with intolerance and bullying, so I fired them."

Seems kind of harsh yet justified at the same time. It is what it is.

"I'm sorry to hear that."

"I guess some people never grow up."

"I don't know if they were quite bullying. It sounded like they were doing their jobs if anything. I've heard that being a cop tends to men testing the limits to one's telling of what happens."

"Are you justifying what they did?"

"I'm saying a bit of ego doesn't hurt but firing someone just because they don't subscribe to your method of being an officer isn't a reason. Now if they had gone with excessive force, that would have been a whole other thing."

"I don't get you."

"And you never will. It is better that way."

"Why are you so against anyone getting close to you?"

"I'm not. I'm against you doing so."

He looks more offended. Sadly his pride is going to be his downfall. I'm sure of it.

With his anger on his face and a hint of hurt, he takes off. It might be for the best.

It's 230 in the morning when I find myself not alone. It is not Charlie. It is a stranger.

"What do you want?" I ask, feeling uneasy.

"3 days," a deep voice says. "Tell him he has 3 days to get the case solved or it is going to get worse."

"For him or who?"

"For you," the voice replies.

When I turn over in bed to see who it is, they are gone.

I don't like it.

I try to get some more rest but it doesn't happen.

Paranoia consumes me. I don't want it. I don't like it. I have no choice. I have to go talk to Charlie. Have to let him know what's going on.

I don't know. Maybe this is a sign. Maybe it is a sign that I have to work with Charlie. That maybe we have to dote on each other deeply. That we might have to spend our days doing this.

I don't know. I'm not cut out to be a cop. I have thought about it. I have looked into it. But I'm just not.

I'm not a coffee addict, donut eating, waiting for problems to arise, and dealing with a melodrama alpha male kind of person.

I'm just not. I prefer to deal with my own things. Live my own life.

No matter how boring some would assume and call it out to be.

19

I get to Charlie that morning looking like a crock of shit. I've showered and such but I've got bags under my eyes from struggling to sleep. The downside of not being used to a town even now.

It sucks. But it is what it is.

I think about getting a counselor. A therapist that I can talk to about anything.

I don't remember if I learned if anyone was a therapist in this town.

I don't know. I'll find out about that later.

"What's going on?" he asks, sounding deeply concerned. And he has reason to be concerned.

I relay the message.

When I am done, he sits back in his chair.

"Son of a bitch. I was hoping this wouldn't happen."

We could hope forever but it won't matter.

"So what do we do?"

"I guess you and I are going to go over everything. I'll call Ernie into this. He is the one that looked over the bodies."

It is smart of him to think that. It would always help in the long run to put things together. To have every mind that had to do something with this case.

Something tells me if we aren't smart and quick about it, we could be in for something that could tear this town apart.

And the last thing anyone wants is for a town to be known for psychopathy and more.

He calls up Ernie and brings him into the office.

This one-room space has to change. A different space would be smart. A space that has more cells or a space that has a bathroom or something because damn.

This looks like one of those old-fashioned school buildings with one big room hosting all 12 grades and one teacher.

It is a sadness that has to be changed.

When he shows up, I meet a man in his forties. I don't recognize him from the welcoming party and that is okay.

Turns out, he is not much for the public eye and being around people. His mind is a bit morbid. Welcome to my world. My mind is quickly becoming that way.

It is hard to not have this kind of mindset when shit like this keeps happening to someone.

"So what do we do?" Ernie asks. His voice is rough yet confident. A sort of ruggedness to it. As if he has been around a lot of smoke lately or maybe because of years of being stuck doing the same job over and over again.

I'm sure it could do a number on someone but still.

Either way, he is something of an honest person. Almost brutally honest like myself.

"Can you catch me up on what you have file wise for the four victims?" I ask.

He nods and speaks it as if it is likely verbatim.

He tells me about how each one has a jagged precision to the cut. How there are odd scratches to the bodies.

The oddities are starting to piece together. The cuts could be from a slight tremor to the body or from nervousness.

The scratches could be defensive wounds or could be from the lack of hygiene when it comes to trimming one's nails. It could be anything or a lot of things.

It is a matter of figuring things out. A question of what could it all mean.

I share my perspective on it. They seem to appreciate it.

What is the word? Perspective isn't what I was shooting for but I'll figure it out in a moment.

It could be a lot of things. I'm not sure yet.

Speculation. That's the word I'm thinking of.

20

There is so much going on that I'm not sure how to feel. I take the time to go with them to the bodies and make observations. I doubt they'll be used but it is something at least.

Sometimes a fresh pair of eyes can do some good, to be after all is said and done.

When I point out some things, Charlie is quick to snap photos on his phone for evidence.

I hope he is printing it out. Evidence on a phone is circumstantial at best. If it's not printed out, it's not even viable. And besides, if there is no lawyer, this town would end up even odder.

"Let me ask this," I ask. "What's up with the justice system? Like is there even a lawyer for this town? A prosecutor or something?"

"Been watching court dramas, have you?" Charlie asks.

"I have not. I haven't touched the damn tube the whole time."

"Then why would you ask such a thing?" Ernie asks.

"Because I live in this town. I should want to know about how it works don't you think?"

Charlie turns to Ernie. "I mean he's not wrong. And if I were to ask him to help me with my work, it would be the least he could learn in response."

I look at the two of them in their bickering glory. The two of them could use some common sense or something. "Ladies!" I exclaim with a whistle. "Care to answer?"

"For the record, we have a prosecutor. Harmony is the best damn prosecutor ever. No personal prejudice. No bias. No holding back. She has manners and tact."

"Would I ever get to meet her?"

"Sometimes it's not the best thing. She works hard and she is hardcore."

"So she could be a bit of fun."

"She is a 7 to 5 kind of girl. After that, she does her own thing. We don't bother her unless she wants to see us."

Fair.

It almost sounds like Charlie is scared of her or intimidated. It makes me want to meet her more.

This woman must have some power over him. Or something that makes her so powerful and intimidating. I like it.

I'm sure at some point or another I will.

I sit back finishing the latest book I've been reading when a knock comes to the door.

I suspect it to be Charlie but it isn't. It is someone so much better.

Not that Charlie is bad in the first place. I just get sick of seeing him all the time. Not that I'm dating him or anything. I'm not into him like that. Or basically at all.

I'm rambling, aren't I?

I swear I have nothing but decent respect for him. I don't see Charlie in that manner. I am just not great at wording things sometimes.

I get to the door and open it to find a woman of a strong frame. I mean confident. Far from frail.

"I'm Harmony. May I come in?"

I nod to her and usher her inside, closing the door behind me.

"How can I help you?"

"You are so mannerly for the new guy. I know most people were worried about that."

I arch a brow at her. What does she mean?

So I ask her to find out.

"I don't mean anything by it. I just have a pulse in this town. I am as friendly as hell. Some people are nervous around me and that's fine."

She is a confident woman of color and holds her own.

And that is great. She is someone that can keep her strength within and hold her cards out in the open. She has no ear. And that is a great quality to have when one is a prosecutor. I don't know what Charlie and Ernie are scared about.

She is great.

"I don't feel a reason to be nervous about you."

"I'm glad to hear it. I am always open to a new friend. Tell me about you, Bob." I smirk and invite her to sit down.

She is a woman of flats. Sensible shoes. Good for her. I don't know why someone would need heels to feel stronger or sexier. Both of those qualities come from within.

I talk to her about myself, answering any questions that I can. When I am done telling her about myself, I wait for it. Some degree of questioning.

"I suspect you think I'm going to question you about the case that you are a witness in. That won't be the case. But if you want to say anything or get anything off your chest regarding it, I won't stop you. I'm not stone cold. I do care about people."

I'm glad to hear it. She has better air about her than Charlie. I get why most people trust her.

"There are some things I do want to mention about the case," I tell her.

She nods and leans forward. No tape recorder like I would expect. No notepad on her person. She must be a steel trap mind kind of person.

Another solid quality.

21

A good hour later, we are sitting back with a glass of wine each and laughing about things. Talking smack on Charlie.

She tells me about her time in town. How she has established herself. This is what good friends make happen.

A glass of wine and some laughs. That's the way it ought to be.

Sometimes it is for the best.

I will be honest. I did forget that I had wine. Someone had dropped it off as a welcome to the town kind of gift.

It is good to share it though. I would be damned if I didn't say I wished this would happen more often.

The more we talk, the more I feel like she and I are going to be best friends.

"So what's it like being a prosecutor?"

"It's nothing like those law shows," she remarks before sipping her wine.

She has relaxed more pulling her hair back into a loose ponytail compared to having it down as she did from the get-go.

"How is it?"

She tells me about how a lot of it is research. How she does not have an assistant. How most people aren't gunning for her or attacking her personal life. It is a very cut and dry kind of thing. She tells me that she is not wanting an assistant. She finds the confidence to work basically on her own.

How she is solid with her work. How she loves it.

And that is great.

"I've been reading your blog," she says.

Oh hell. Why is that something that is a little worrisome for people to bring up for me?

"Okay?"

"I love it. You tell it like it is. Let me know if you ever need recommendations."

"Why? Do you think there is a lack of reviews or shoutouts to books in the world?

"Aside from teen books? Hell yes. People of color need more representation. Now I know you are not a person of color but it would still be nice to see more love in that department."

I wouldn't mind it. I'm not one to shy from anything. I always love a good diversity. It is nice to know that someone would be interested in it.

Besides, it could be a great step in the right direction.

"I'll look into it."

"I appreciate that."

We chat for a bit longer before she calls for a ride and starts for the door.

"This was fun. We might have to do it again," I remark.

"Oh, we will. I haven't had this much fun in a long while."

We share a hug and she heads out to her ride.

I get some rest that night and wonder what more could come on the horizon. Good, I hope.

We still have 2 days until the deadline. Progress is being made. I'm sure of it.

The next afternoon, Ernie, Charlie, and Harmony meet up at my house. We work towards figuring things out. Walking around in the backyard that hasn't been cut because you know, location of evidence at one point. It is what it is.

I suspect it is going to be a bitch and a half. The lot of us talk about everything that we can. It comes to a point when Harmony starts taking notes while pacing back and forth. She is quick to type up the notes on her phone.

Look at her being progressive. I love how quick this town is with tech. How they are eager to embrace it.

When we are working on figuring things out loud, she switches her notes over to her iPad and puts her own notes on it.

She is good about everything. I know for a fact she had to save up for a year to get that iPad.

She is like me, something of a humble person with a means to work hard and maybe reward once in a while.

It makes me all the more grateful for the deal I have with Terry. This town is coming around for me big time.

It is a matter of time.

22

I suspect we are missing something. Something right under our noses and we have no damn clue.

What is it?

We have been looking at the victim but...son of a bitch!

That's what we haven't been doing.

Psychological profile of who could be doing this.

That would be a ticket. And with time slowly becoming that whole thing and a half, it would be smart.

It is a matter of time.

Christ and a half. Why didn't I think of that sooner?

Why didn't any of us think of that?

I'm not going to belittle Harmony because she has a lot on her shoulders but come on.

I grab a legal pad and start taking simple notes.

"What's up?" Harmony and Charlie ask as they see me staring at the legal pad.

"We haven't been thinking on one part of this case and with time rapidly coming upon us, I'm trying to figure it out."

"Psych profile?" Charlie asks.

"Yeah. Have you ever considered it?"

"Nope."

Of course not. "Typical men. Never thinking about how someone could be in a case. They just want to lock up someone and feel superior. What do you have?" Harmony remarks.

I share with her my remarks. My thoughts. She nods and adds her own notes on the computer.

"This does seem odd. Why warn you of a deadline? Why expect to be the center of attention? There seems to be a degree of narcissism. Not to mention a sadistic nature."

Right to the point.

That is the way it ought to be. Maybe Charlie ought to take a lesson or two on it.

Something about it makes a person all the better.

I don't know what it is.

Another day goes by. This is not going well. The deadline is coming in fast. By midnight tonight, it is either going to go very well or very badly.

"I have a plan in mind," Charlie says as he walks into the house. I wish some people would administer the common sense to knock.

That would be nice. If I had been naked, this could've been awkward.

Even with his powers over me with four coffees in hand, I suspect this won't save him.

"What do you have in mind?" I ask, ignoring the gnawing need to rip him a new one for bursting into my house.

He might be a sheriff but he is a human being. And I figured he would have some common decency.

I guess not.

He tells me of the plan and when he is done, I don't know if I want to hug him or knock the hell out of him.

If not for the coffee he brings, I would've knocked him in the frigging head. No doubt about it.

What I am not a fan of is having to wait until the right time.

Or maybe I should contact Harmony and see if she has another plan.

Got to say, I'm not a fan of being the bait but somehow it doesn't seem to matter.

It is going to happen at some point or another, I suspect.

A few hours later, Charlie is gone and I call up Harmony. She is a breath of fresh air. Due to our phones of choice, we are quick to facetime switch.

"So what's the plan that Charlie has come up with?" she asks. She is sipping at her soda while I'm sipping at the third of four coffees.

I tell her what he has in mind and she chokes on her soda for a moment before forcing it down.

"Is he out of his mind?"

I shrug. "That seems to be his plan in mind."

"Well, I'll be giving him a talking to. Better yet, hold on," she says.

I see her fingers dance on the screen and soon he pops up on his phone. He is sitting back in his office.

"What's up?" he asks.

"Are you insane? You don't make a witness bait. That is how we end up losing a case from the get-go. You have to be dumber than a sack of hammers Charles Handleman."

Handleman? That's his last name? Guess you can learn a lot about someone through a bit of a rant.

But it makes sense. I mean, I am not one for my last name. I don't know what it is about the name Hopeful but too many people have looked at me oddly.

Robert Hopeful. That's my name. Don't bother asking about it. I don't know what the hell went through my parent's minds. Marie and John Hopeful were some peculiar people. I love them to bits but damn.

Getting back to the matter at hand, I wait for it. For some sort of chance to speak up but I wait for her to be done with her rant at him.

He looks at me. "Way to go."

"Don't you dare chide him for something that you did. Did you think about it in all aspects? Or did you think, 'oh, hey. The killer contacted and stalked him, why not use him to lure the bastard out?'" I am sure I can see a vein sticking out of her head.

Charlie is redder than a beet. And to me, it's hard not to chuckle at him getting his ass chewed like he is getting scolded by his mama.

"Boy, you better be thankful we are in this call or I would call your mama."

"Harmony. We grew up next door to each other in this town. Basin is a simple place. I figured it would be smart to lure them out."

"And what? You would get an eyeful and a half of Bob while you are at it? Good god man!"

23

"Now that we have that bullshit out of the way, what do you suggest we do?" Charlie asks.

"Maybe we look at what we know from each person in town in the database and narrow down who it could be. Capture them before nightfall. Stop them before they start more hell."

It makes a solid bit of sense. And she is nothing if not honest about the way it ought to be. The way I see it, everything's coming together in its own way. A more solid plan."

"We don't have days. We have hours before it happens. Do you have a quicker method?"

"When was the last time you updated your computer?" she asks.

"What are you talking about? Big Bailey is working just fine."

"Yeah, okay," she snorts.

"What? She has been solid for me forever."

"You've had her 10 years. She needs to be updated. How long does it take you to open an email?"

This back and forth between the two of them is so delectably sweet. I cannot get enough of it.

"Seconds."

"On the computer, dumbass."

He is quiet for a moment.

That much says it all. If there is anything to be said about the male species, it is that it is clear they are guilty of something or that they don't want to answer for fear of self-incrimination when it comes to being wrong. It is a pride thing.

"That's what I thought. I'm coming over to the office. I'll swing by and pick you up, Bob. we can head over and look through it all. I'll bring my iPad for us to use while we update that monster, he has behind him," she chuckles.

"Sounds good. I'll see you soon," I remark and hang up.

I get ready and dive into the fourth coffee before heading out the door to wait for her.

I don't expect her to have a motorcycle. Not a motorcycle. Wait, what is the name of three-wheel motorcycles? Trikes. That's the word.

She pulls up on one. That sucker gives enough space for a lot of ass. And I'm not exactly tight on the tush.

She takes my drink and sets it on the cup holder while I get on.

"If you need it, let me know."

"I'll tell you."

I look over her shoulder to find she has a smoothie. The girl has been on it like ever.

"Do you make your own or do you go somewhere?"

"I'll show you the place on the way to the office," she remarks.

She hands back my drink as I am strapped in and takes off. She occasionally sips at her drink.

She pulls up to the smoothie shop. "This is the place that I get mine. They make good stuff. Many different flavors. Smooth blending and more. It is worth it."

How did I not notice this place before?

I don't know but it is on the other side of Nina's shop.

"Mind if I stop in Nina's shop. I'm sure we could all use a bite for the work we have ahead of us."

"I like the way you think."

"Wow. I'm not sure I am glad you came with these or offended," Charlie says as he sees 3 boxes of delights. One box is donuts that I got for him. One box is sandwich bites--which I will say I didn't know Nina made but turns out she is working on incorporating into her menu which is great because not everyone needs sweets all the time--and the last box is pastries with fruit filling in them.

I didn't know someone could stuff croissants and rolls with fruit filling but she has done it.

"Are you really getting butthurt about him bringing a variety of things?"

"I'm more hurt about the donuts part."

"You could use a few pounds anyway," she says and pats at his stomach as he comes over to the 3 open boxes.

Then she walks around. "Never mind."

She is as catty as ever. I love it.

I bust out laughing at her statement.

24

We munch down after starting the large collection of updates his computer needs to do.

We get down and dirty with focus. We are hardcore writing shit on white board. Eliminating people that couldn't be the case.

It comes down to a handful of people after several hours. We don't have much for time. I look at my phone.

I have 2 hours at least. That's it.

"We need to do something quick. Time is of the essence."

"I guess we have no choice but to take Charlie's plan and make it happen. I hate it but this shit has to stop."

The way I see it, the sooner it is done, the better off things are.

And the sooner we can catch the son of a bitch.

Getting to the house, I have a meal and get to bed. I don't have a good feeling in my stomach. I know Charlie is nearby but really.

Good thing I know how to hold my own. I know how to fight back if I have to.

I shut my brain off and start to relax in bed.

The night seems to go at a snail's pace. I'm not a fan of it. I suspect my nerves are going to get the best of me. I feel my stomach starting to do flips. I don't know if it is nerves or because dinner doesn't agree. I suspect nerves are causing the second part. That could be the case.

Either way, it will be done.

A few hours pass and I'm starting to finally conk out when they slip in. The rough male deep voice chuckles.

"I thought you would've had it done by now. That you would've caught me."

Charlie comes out, cocking his gun. "We just did," he smirks. He whips out the cuffs and slams the bastard into a wall. So much for not having property damage. I guess that is unavoidable in this case.

"I think not," the guy says and starts to shove Charlie back.

I'm quick to slip out of bed and help out. I grab the bastard and pin him hard while Charlie manages to cough him.

And yes, I know it is a male.

Charlie is quick to flick the lights on so we can see who it is.

No shit.

It is one of the former cops. Someone that chose to vigorously question me. And now it makes sense.

They were wanting deep details. As if it is something erotic to them.

And that is worrisome to me. Someone seems to have a sort of gruesome love. I wonder why I didn't bother to piece that together the whole time.

I begin to question a lot of things.

I don't know. Maybe I have been too lost in my own head.

"Send a text to Harmony. Tell her we caught the bastard. Then I'll treat you to a breakfast or a late-night snack or something," Charlie says.

"I'm on it."

25

A few months later

I'm sitting back and reading into an amazing teen book after finishing one that blew my mind.

I have never had my mind blown as much as the last book I read by a new author. Holy hellfire.

It is a great read and I share a review on my blog. My blog is still blowing up. People are visiting it and dropping donations like no tomorrow. I feel so grateful to hell.

People continue to surprise. Even when times are tough for people that are struggling, they still manage to donate a buck or two.

And to me, that is what makes it all worth it. Not the money but the surprises of people.

Most people are selfish as hell.

And don't get me wrong, I am far from the perfect person.

I still have my vices--coffee. But I do my best to make sure that people get some love. Terry is at a familiar level with me that they are texting me when they get new books in.

Some authors are coming in to sign books every now and then. It is nice to see that.

It is a matter of coming around. People are starting to acknowledge all of it.

Finishing the book, I crank out a review and hit post on it.

I don't know what it is but these days people are putting out some damn good stuff. I'm still inhaling books like coffee.

I don't have a problem, I can stop when I want.

Harmony comes to check on me. She slyly drops a couple books onto my coffee table.

"Just for a read or two."

I laugh. "I'll make sure to dive into them soon."

She smirks. "I know you will. You are quick about that."

I shrug. "I try."

"Just keep up the good work."

"I plan on it."

"So let me ask this. Are you planning on helping out Charlie more?"

"I know he dotes on me from time to time but I don't know if I could ever do that full time. That could be on just him."

She nods. "I don't blame you. This is not something for everyone."

That is the ultimate understatement.

"So are you busy at the moment?"

"Not at the moment. Just finished a few goodies."

She glances at the covers. "I might have to borrow them."

"As long as you use a bookmark and don't fold pages, I'm sold."

She laughs. "I don't do that dark alley shit. I treat books like they are gems." And that is because they are. Someone has put a lot of fucking time into them and works under pressure for that bad boy.

So you better believe someone could and should see them as gems.

This town is becoming my warm blanket. My comfort. I cannot begin to describe how much I am in love with this town. It's interesting and quaint people. The way people embrace each other and look out for each other.

A person would have to be a fool to try and destroy what is going on. But I have much to learn about this town.

I have much to learn about how it came to be but something tells me I am going to be in for quite the long ride. And I'm ready. I'll gladly strap in and see where it takes me.

The end